Suggestions for Parents

First, read the book to your child. Allow him or her all the time needed to look closely at the pictures and to discuss the story. Then—even on another day—read the story again, now pointing to the words as you read them. After a few readings, the child who is ready to read will begin to pick up the often-repeated words—even the big ones! Before long (there's no hurry) the child will try to read the book alone. It is most important that you patiently build your child's confidence and give him or her the sense that reading is fun. You will find that there is nothing to match the excitement and satisfaction your child will feel on learning to read *a whole book*!

Where Did That Naughty Little Hamster Go?

By Patty Wolcott
Illustrated by
Rosekrans Hoffman

Random House 🏠 New York

Library of Congress Cataloging-in-Publication Data
Wolcott, Patty.
    Where did that naughty little hamster go? / by Patty Wolcott ;
illustrated by Rosekrans Hoffman.
        Originally published: Reading, Mass. : Addison-Wesley, 1974.
            p.   cm. — (Ten-word readers)
        Summary: A group of first graders search their classroom
for their missing hamster.
        ISBN 0-679-81924-X (trade) — ISBN 0-679-91924-4 (lib. bdg.)
        [1. Hamsters—Fiction. 2. Lost and found possessions—Fiction.]
I. Hoffman, Rosekrans, ill.   II. Title.   III. Series: Wolcott, Patty.
Ten-word readers.
        PZ7.W8185Wh   1991   [E]—dc20   91-12133

Manufactured in the United States of America
10 9 8 7 6 5 4 3 2 1

naughty little hamster go?

Where did that little
Charlie Hamster go?

Charlie Hamster!

Here's that little hamster.

That naughty hamster!

CLOTH SCRAPS

Dear little Charlie Hamster.